ARTFOLDS

....

This book belongs to

....

Folded by

Color Editions No. 4

MOM

featuring

The Magic of Mom:
Wise Words About the Wonders of Motherhood

Studio Fun Books
White Plains, New York • Montréal, Québec • Bath, United Kingdom

ArtFolds
Color Editions No. 4
Mom

ArtFolds is a patent-pending process.

ISBN 978-0-7944-3334-5

To learn more about ArtFolds, visit www.artfolds.com

Customized and/or prefolded ArtFolds are available. To explore options
and pricing, email specialorder@artfolds.com.

To discover the wide range of products available from Studio Fun
International, visit www.studiofun.com

Address any comments about ArtFolds to:
Publisher
Studio Fun Books
44 South Broadway, 7th floor
White Plains, NY 10601

Or send an email to publisher@artfolds.com.

Printed in China
Conforms to ASTM F963

1 3 5 7 9 10 8 6 4 2   LPP/10/14

About ArtFolds

THE BOOK YOU HOLD in your hands is more than just a book. It's an ArtFolds™! Inside are simple instructions that will show you how to fold the pages to transform this book into a beautiful sculpture. No special skill is required; all you'll do is carefully fold the corners of marked book pages, based on the folding lines provided. When complete, you'll have created a long-lasting work of art. It's fun and easy, and can be completed in just one evening!

To add to the experience, each ArtFolds contains compelling reading content. In this edition, you'll share in the joys of motherhood as expressed by mothers and their children over the years.

Each ArtFolds edition is designed by an established, professional book sculptor whose works are routinely displayed and sold in art galleries, museum shops, and online crafts and art stores. ArtFolds celebrates this community of artists and encourages you to support this expanding art form by seeking out their work and sharing their unique designs and creations with others.

To learn more about ArtFolds, visit www.artfolds.com. There you'll find details of all ArtFolds™ editions, instructional videos, and much more.

Instructions

Creating your ArtFolds Color Editions book sculpture is easy! Just follow these simple instructions and guidelines:

1. Always fold right-hand pages.

2. Always fold toward you.

3. All folding pages require two folds: the top corner will fold down, and the bottom corner will fold up.

1, 2

4. Grasp the top right corner of the page, and fold until the side of the page aligns exactly with the TOP of the horizontal color bar.

4

5. Grasp the bottom right corner of the page, and fold upward until the side of the page aligns exactly with the BOTTOM of the horizontal color bar.

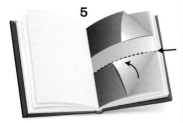
5

6. Carefully run your finger across the folds to make sure they are straight, crisp, and accurate.

7. Continue on to the next page and repeat until your ArtFolds book sculpture is complete!

Extra advice

- We recommend washing and then thoroughly drying your hands prior to folding.

- Some folders prefer using a tool to help make fold lines straight and sharp. Bone folders, metal rulers, popsicle sticks, or any other firm, straight tool will work.

- Some folders prefer to rotate their book sideways to make folding easier.

- Remember: The more accurate you are with each fold, the more accurate your completed book sculpture will be!

Folding begins in just four pages!

For more folding instructions and videos, visit www.artfolds.com

The Magic of Mom

Wise Words About the Wonders of Motherhood

Edited by Stephanie Schwartz

JOYOUS. FUNNY. PROFOUNDLY SATISFYING. THOROUGHLY ENRICHING. For all the countless challenges of motherhood, the pleasures of raising a child are among the greatest on Earth, only rivaled by the child's deep contentment in being so loved. The role demands the very best of women, and that is instinctively what they provide. Mothers are teachers, carers, leaders, and healers. With every meal, hug, and word, mothers create the future every day for our children.

Equally wondrous is how each woman's path as a mother is as unique as the child being raised. So many writers, thinkers, and personalities, for so many centuries, have attempted to put into words what they feel in their hearts about being a mom, or being loved by one. Their words speak both to the universal truths of motherhood, as well as to each woman's personal journey, joys, and travails.

The Magic of Mom has gathered these wise words within its pages, weaving among them just a few of the countless reasons we can all be thankful for our moms and for the experience of motherhood. Here is a celebration of this most special bond—for the mother you are, the mother you love, or the mother you're going to become.

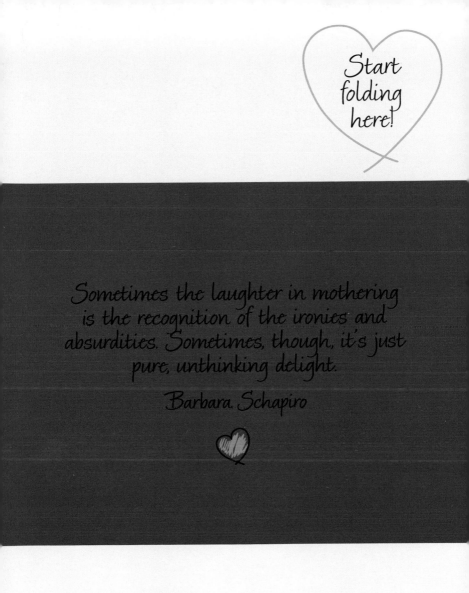

Start folding here!

Sometimes the laughter in mothering is the recognition of the ironies and absurdities. Sometimes, though, it's just pure, unthinking delight.

Barbara Schapiro

When you are a mother, you are never really alone in your thoughts. A mother always has to think twice, once for herself and once for her child.

Sophia Loren

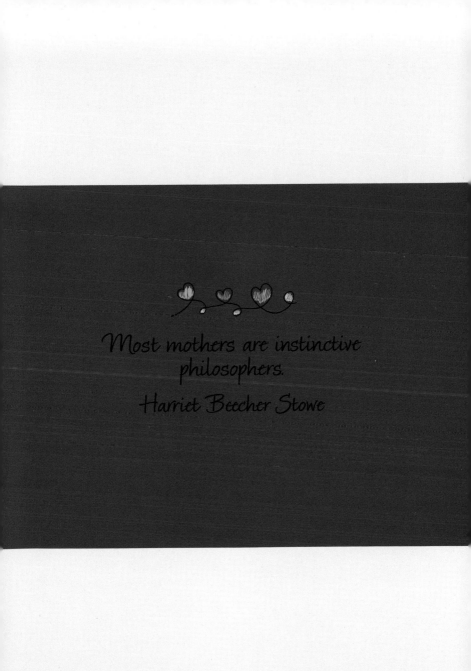

Most mothers are instinctive
philosophers.

Harriet Beecher Stowe

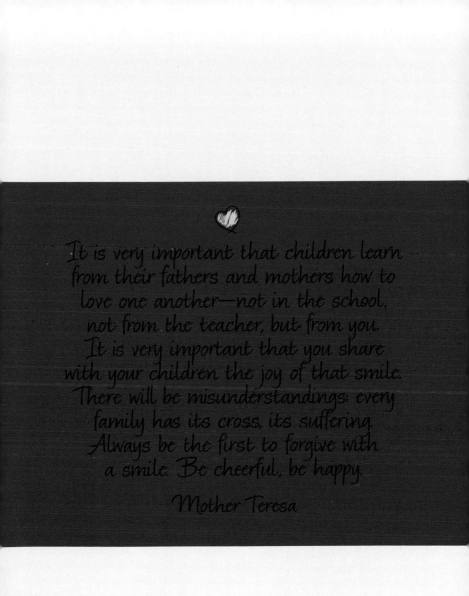

It is very important that children learn
from their fathers and mothers how to
love one another—not in the school,
not from the teacher, but from you.
It is very important that you share
with your children the joy of that smile.
There will be misunderstandings; every
family has its cross, its suffering.
Always be the first to forgive with
a smile. Be cheerful, be happy.

Mother Teresa

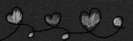

When you were small, your cupped palms
each held a candleworth under the skin,
enough light to begin,
and as you grew,
light gathered in you. . .

Carol Ann Duffy

There was never a child so lovely but his mother was glad to get him to sleep.

Ralph Waldo Emerson

A man loves his sweetheart the most, his
wife the best, but his mother the longest.

Irish proverb

Some mothers are kissing mothers
and some are scolding mothers, but it
is love just the same, and most mothers
kiss and scold together.

Pearl S. Buck

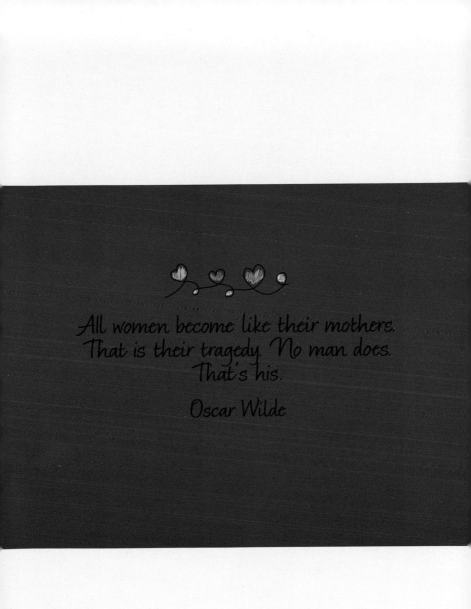

All women become like their mothers.
That is their tragedy. No man does.
That's his.

Oscar Wilde

Biology is the least of what makes
someone a mother.

Oprah Winfrey

A mother's happiness is like a beacon,
lighting up the future
but reflected also in the past
in the guise of fond memories.

Honoré de Balzac

More than in any other human
relationship, overwhelmingly more,
motherhood means being instantly
interruptible, responsive, and responsible.

Tillie Olsen

To nourish children and raise them against the odds is any time, any place, more valuable than to fix bolts in cars or design nuclear weapons.

Marilyn French

When your mother asks, "Do you want
a piece of advice?" it is a mere formality.
It doesn't matter if you answer yes or no.
You're going to get it anyway.

Erma Bombeck

Woman is the salvation or the destruction of the family. She carries its destiny in the folds of her mantle.

Henri-Frédéric Amiel

Thanks, Mom,
for being the gravitational center
of our family.

Thanks, Mom,
for always being in my corner.

The angels, whispering to one another,
Can find, among their
burning terms of love,
None so devotional as that of "Mother"...

Edgar Allan Poe

'I have no name;
I am but two days old.'
What shall I call thee?
'I happy am,
Joy is my name.'
Sweet joy befall thee!

William Blake

I'm thankful motherhood gives me more
to laugh about than cry about.

If I have done anything
in my life worth attention,
I feel sure that I inherited the
disposition from my mother.

Booker T. Washington

A mother is not a person to lean on,
but a person to make leaning unnecessary.

Dorothy Canfield Fisher

Men are what their mothers made them.
Ralph Waldo Emerson

By and large, mothers and housewives are the only workers who do not have regular time off. They are the great vacationless class.

Anne Morrow Lindbergh

Motherhood: All love begins
and ends there.

Robert Browning

If I were damned of body and soul,
I know whose prayers would make me whole,
Mother o' mine, O mother o' mine.

Rudyard Kipling

I love you, Mother, I have
woven a wreath
Of rhymes wherewith to crown
your honored name:
In you not fourscore years
can dim the flame
Of love, whose blessed glow
transcends the laws
Of time and change and mortal
life and death.

Christina Rossetti

Time does not really exist for mothers,
with regard to their children.
It does not matter greatly how old the
child is—in the blink of an eye, a mother
can see the child again as they were
when they were born, when they learned
how to walk, as they were at any age—
any time, even when the child is fully
grown or a parent themselves.

Diana Gabaldon

I'm thankful motherhood
encourages me to revisit some of
my favorite books.

There is no way to be a perfect mother,
and a million ways to be a good one.

Jill Churchill

Mothers and their children are in a category all their own. There's no bond so strong in the entire world. No love so instantaneous and forgiving.

Gail Tsukiyama

I'm thankful
motherhood
lets me rediscover
the pleasures of the
playground.

I'm thankful motherhood shows me the
wonder in the flight of a ladybug,
the petals of a dandelion, the colors
in a soap bubble.

It is as grandmothers that our mothers
come into the fullness of their grace.

Christopher Morley

Thanks, Mom,
for always
answering the
hard questions.

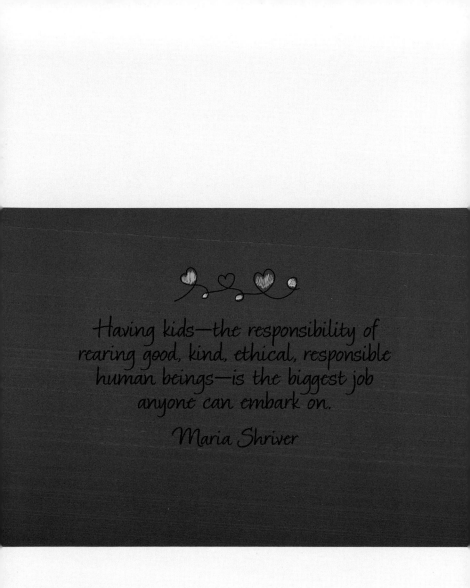

Having kids—the responsibility of
rearing good, kind, ethical, responsible
human beings—is the biggest job
anyone can embark on.

Maria Shriver

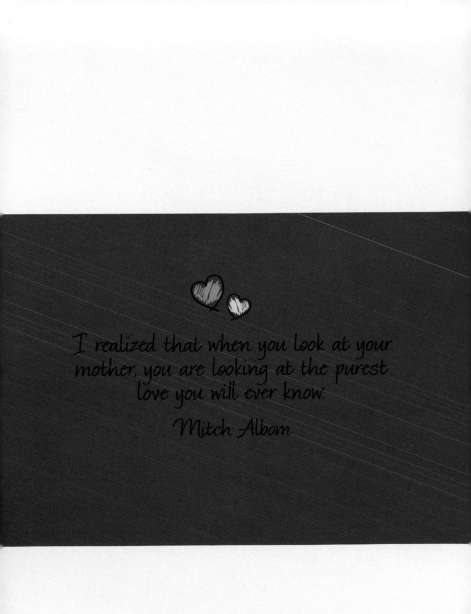

I realized that when you look at your mother, you are looking at the purest love you will ever know.

Mitch Albom

The mother's heart is
the child's schoolroom.

Henry Ward Beecher

Thanks, Mom,
for keeping a box of my favorite cookies
in the house—and two boxes during
exam times!

I'm thankful motherhood is
a wondrous journey.

I learned from my mother
how to love the living ...

Julia Kasdorf

So for the mother's sake
the child was dear,
And dearer was the mother for the child.

Samuel Taylor Coleridge

Mother is the name for God in the lips
and hearts of little children.

William Makepeace Thackeray

Children and mothers never truly part,
Bound in the beating of each other's hearts.

Charlotte Gray

Any mother could perform the jobs of several air traffic controllers with ease.

♥ Lisa Alther

I'm thankful motherhood
teaches me new things about
the world every day.

Mama exhorted her children at every
opportunity to "jump at de sun."
We might not land on the sun, but
at least we would get off the ground.

Zora Neale Hurston

Thanks, Mom, for curling up on the couch
with me to read my favorite book.

The strength of motherhood is
greater than natural laws.

Barbara Kingsolver

I'm thankful motherhood keeps me
on my toes.

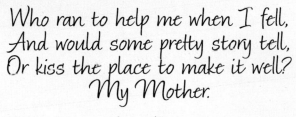

Who ran to help me when I fell,
And would some pretty story tell,
Or kiss the place to make it well?
My Mother.

Ann Taylor

A mother's arms are more comforting
than anyone else's.

Diana, Princess of Wales

The mother loves her child most divinely, not when she surrounds him with comfort and anticipates his wants, but when she resolutely holds him to the highest standards and is content with nothing less than his best.

Hamilton Wright Mabie

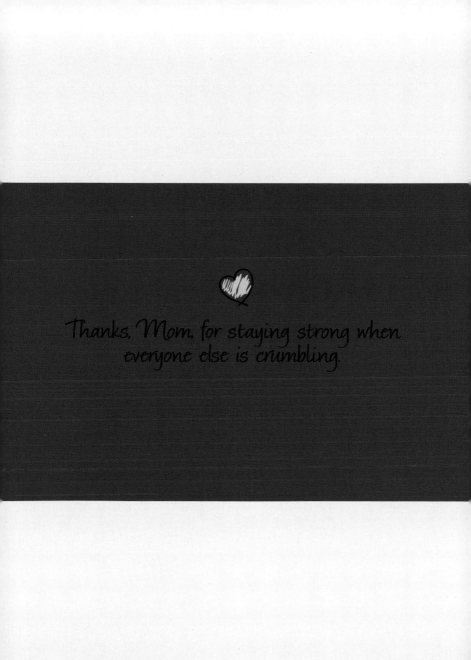

Thanks, Mom, for staying strong when everyone else is crumbling.

Being a mother is an attitude,
not a biological relation.

Robert A. Heinlein

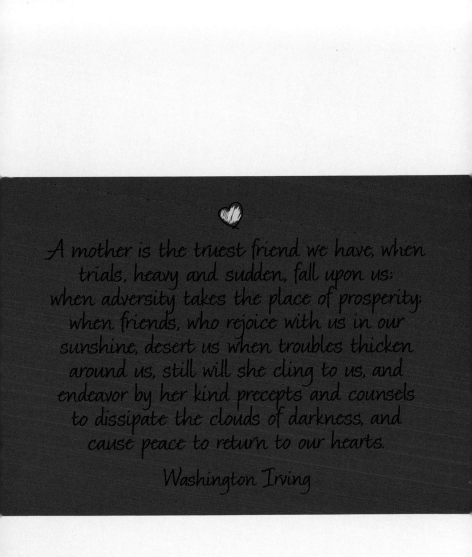

A mother is the truest friend we have, when
trials, heavy and sudden, fall upon us;
when adversity takes the place of prosperity;
when friends, who rejoice with us in our
sunshine, desert us when troubles thicken
around us, still will she cling to us, and
endeavor by her kind precepts and counsels
to dissipate the clouds of darkness, and
cause peace to return to our hearts.

Washington Irving

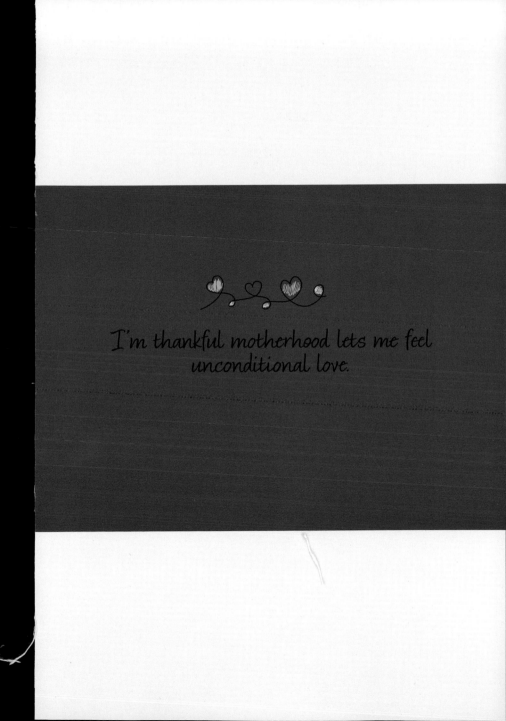

I'm thankful motherhood lets me feel
unconditional love.

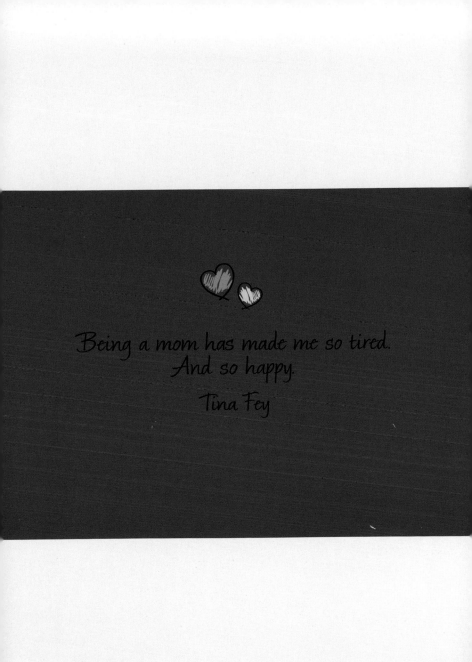

Being a mom has made me so tired.
And so happy.

Tina Fey

Thanks, Mom, for teaching me to be
as courageous as you are.

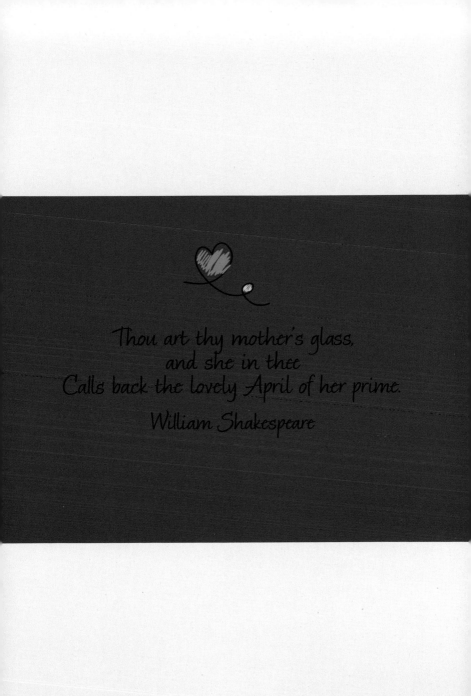

Thou art thy mother's glass,
and she in thee
Calls back the lovely April of her prime.

William Shakespeare

I'm thankful motherhood gives me the
gift of watching my children grow.

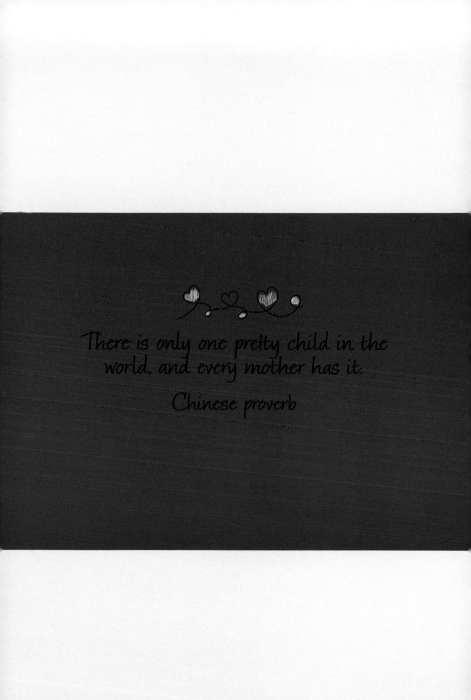

There is only one pretty child in the
world, and every mother has it.

Chinese proverb

Those helpless bundles of power and promise that come into our world show us our true selves—who we are, who we are not, who we wish we could be.

Hillary Rodham Clinton

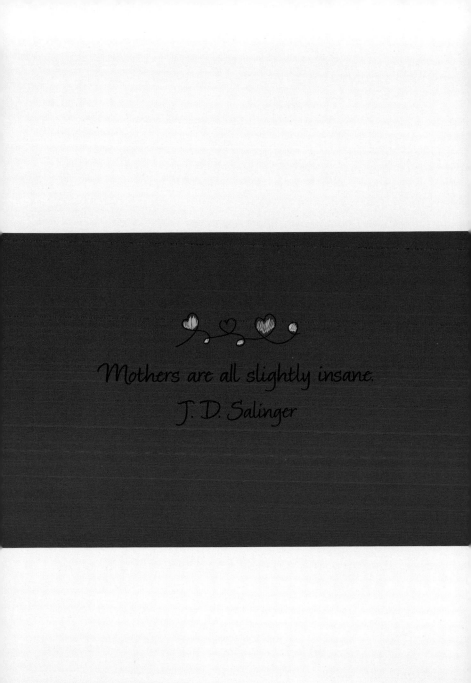

Mothers are all slightly insane.

J. D. Salinger

Women know
The way to rear up children (to be just)
They know a simple, merry, tender knack
Of tying sashes, fitting baby-shoes,
And stringing pretty words
that make no sense,
And kissing full sense into empty words.

Elizabeth Barrett Browning

Thanks, Mom, for being the magic glue
in my messy life.

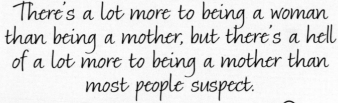

There's a lot more to being a woman
than being a mother, but there's a hell
of a lot more to being a mother than
most people suspect.

Roseanne Barr

I'm thankful motherhood makes me
live in the moment.

There was never a great man
who had not a great mother—it is
hardly an exaggeration.

Olive Schreiner

Thanks, Mom, for letting me know
you're proud of me. I'm proud of you, too!

The heart of a mother is a deep abyss
at the bottom of which you will always
find forgiveness.

Honoré de Balzac

I'm thankful motherhood allows me
to be both silly and strong.

Becoming a mother makes you the mother of all children. From now on each wounded, abandoned, frightened child is yours. You live in the suffering mothers of every race and creed and weep with them. You long to comfort all who are desolate.

Charlotte Gray

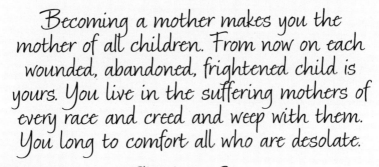

Thanks, Mom, for being patient
when I'm being impossible.

I'm thankful motherhood
makes me feel so alive.

Where the city of the best-bodied
mothers stands,
There the great city stands.

Walt Whitman

To describe my mother would be to write about a hurricane in its perfect power. Or the climbing, falling colors of a rainbow.

Maya Angelou

Thanks, Mom, for the millions of amazing hugs that never fail to make me feel better.

I'm thankful motherhood teaches me
what real patience is.

A mother's arms are made of tenderness
and children sleep soundly in them.

Victor Hugo

The natural state of motherhood is
unselfishness. When you become a mother,
you are no longer the center of the universe.
You relinquish that position to your children.

Jessica Lange

Thanks, Mom,
for being the best role model ever.

As is the mother, so is her daughter.

Ezekiel 16:44

I'm thankful motherhood stretches
my creativity and ingenuity.

Congrats!
You're half-
way there!

It will be gone before you know it.
The fingerprints on the wall appear higher
and higher and then they disappear.

Dorothy Evslin

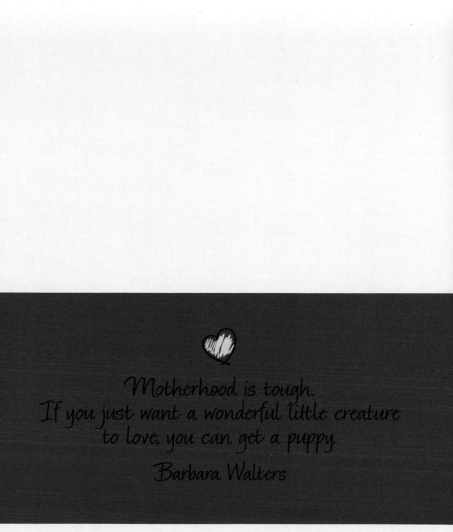

Motherhood is tough.
If you just want a wonderful little creature
to love, you can get a puppy.

Barbara Walters

Thanks, Mom,
for nagging me to do my homework—
as I've grown up, I understand why.

Everybody wants to save the earth;
nobody wants to help
Mom with the dishes.

P. J. O'Rourke

I'm thankful motherhood
opens my heart.

God knows that a mother needs fortitude and courage and tolerance and flexibility and patience and firmness and nearly every other brave aspect of the human soul. But because I happen to be a parent of almost fiercely maternal nature, I praise casualness. It seems to me the rarest of virtues. It is useful enough when children are small. It is useful to the point of necessity when they are adolescents.

Phyllis McGinley

My mother taught me about the power
of inspiration and courage, and she
did it with a strength and a passion
I wish could be bottled.

Carly Fiorina

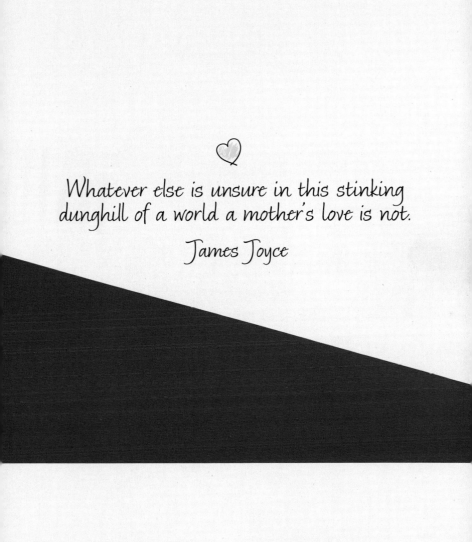

Whatever else is unsure in this stinking
dunghill of a world a mother's love is not.

James Joyce

The mother-child relationship is paradoxical and, in a sense, tragic. It requires the most intense love on the mother's side, yet this very love must help the child grow away from the mother and to become fully independent.

Erich Fromm

I'm thankful motherhood is
such a crazy adventure.

I'm thankful motherhood has secret joys
known only to me and my child.

Thanks, Mom, for letting me learn the
hard way even when you already
knew the easy way.

And so our mothers and grandmothers have, more often than not anonymously, handed on the creative spark, the seed of the flower they themselves never hoped to see—or like a sealed letter they could not plainly read.

Alice Walker

Thanks, Mom, for sticking by me
and being my best friend.

Love as powerful as your mother's
for you leaves its own mark ... to have
been loved so deeply ... will give us
some protection forever.

J. K. Rowling

I'm thankful motherhood is unpredictable.

Hundreds of dewdrops to greet the dawn,
Hundreds of bees in the purple clover,
Hundreds of butterflies on the lawn,
But only one mother the wide world over.

George Cooper

I am sure that if the mothers
of various nations could meet, there would
be no more wars.

E. M. Forster

Thanks, Mom, for being so generous
with your time and energy.

I'm thankful motherhood gives me
an excuse to build snowmen and run
through sprinklers again.

♡

I think it's worth trying to be a mother
who delights in who her children are, in their
knock-knock jokes and earnest questions.
A mother who spends less time obsessing
about what will happen, or what has
happened, and more time reveling in what is.

Ayelet Waldman

Completeness? Happiness? These words
don't come close to describing my emotions.
There truly is nothing I can say to
capture what motherhood means to me ...

Anita Baker

Thanks, Mom,

for being able to keep a secret.

What children take from us, they give ...
we become people who feel more deeply,
question more deeply, hurt more
deeply, and love more deeply.

Sonia Taitz

Thanks, Mom, for listening to all my
news, good and bad.

I'm thankful motherhood changes me
for the better (almost) every day.

I looked on child rearing not only as a work of love and duty but as a profession that was fully as interesting and challenging as any honorable profession in the world and one that demanded the best I could bring to it.

Rose Kennedy

My mother had a slender, small body,
but a large heart. A heart so large that
everybody's joys found welcome in it, and
hospitable accommodation.

Mark Twain

I'm thankful motherhood reintroduced
hopscotch and jump rope to my life.

Great mothers
build bridges instead of walls.

Reed Markham

Thanks, Mom, for kissing away the boo-boos.

I remember my mother's prayers
and they have always followed me.
They have clung to me all my life.

Abraham Lincoln

I'm thankful that motherhood reminds me that doing my best is more than good enough.

Motherhood has completely changed me.
It's just about the most completely
humbling experience I've ever had.

Diane Keaton

Yes, Mother. I can see you are flawed.
You have not hidden it.
That is your greatest gift to me.

Alice Walker

Thanks, Mom, for sharing your passions
with me and teaching me to develop my own.

I'm thankful motherhood slows
down the pace of my life some
days and speeds it immeasurably
on others.

A baby is God's opinion that
the world should go on.

Carl Sandburg

I'm thankful motherhood opens
so many doors for me.

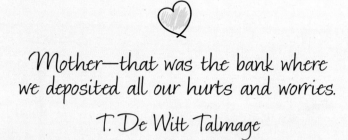

Mother—that was the bank where
we deposited all our hurts and worries.

T. De Witt Talmage

Motherhood brings as much joy as ever, but it still brings boredom, exhaustion, and sorrow, too. Nothing else ever will make you as happy or as sad, as proud or as tired, for nothing is quite as hard as helping a person develop his own individuality especially while you struggle to keep your own.

Marguerite Kelly and Elia Parsons

Thanks, Mom, for showing me how
to live every day to its fullest.

No matter how old a mother is,
she watches her middle-aged children
for signs of improvement.

Florida Scott-Maxwell

Life began with waking up
and loving my mother's face.

George Eliot

Thanks, Mom, for knowing
when something really is wrong even
though I tell you everything is fine.

Whatever your age, having a strong female to look up to and learn from is priceless—and for that we thank our mothers wholeheartedly.

Sarah Bailey

Thanks, Mom, for being the loudest
and most loving cheerleader
at every one of my games.

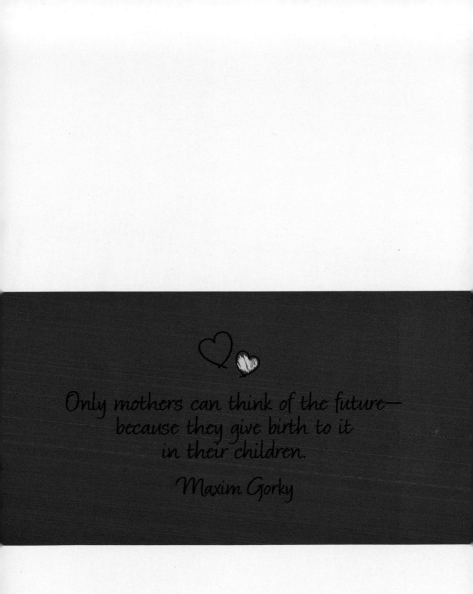

Only mothers can think of the future—
because they give birth to it
in their children.

Maxim Gorky

Thanks, Mom, for being the guiding
force in our family's life.

As it stands, motherhood is a sort of
wilderness through which each woman
hacks her way, part martyr, part pioneer ...

Rachel Cusk

Thanks, Mom, for waking me up with
a smile and a bowl of hot oatmeal on
the coldest winter mornings.

The real religion of the world comes from
women much more than from men—
from mothers most of all, who carry
the key of our souls in their bosoms.

Oliver Wendell Holmes

One good mother is worth a hundred schoolmasters.

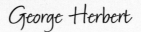

George Herbert

Making a decision to have a child—
it's momentous. It is to decide forever
to have your heart go walking around
outside your body.

Elizabeth Stone

Grown don't mean nothing to a mother.
A child is a child. They get bigger, older, but
grown? In my heart it don't mean a thing.

Toni Morrison

Motherhood is a choice you make every day, to put someone else's happiness and well-being ahead of your own, to teach the hard lessons, to do the right thing even when you're not sure what the right thing is ... and to forgive yourself, over and over again, for doing everything wrong.

Donna Ball

God could not be everywhere,
so he created mothers.

Jewish proverb

No one in the world can take the place of your mother. Right or wrong, from her viewpoint you are always right. She may scold you for little things, but never for the big ones.

Harry Truman

Thanks, Mom, for always knowing
where my favorite T-shirt is.

A wise parent humors the desire
for independent action, so as to become
the friend and advisor when his absolute
rule shall cease.

—Elizabeth Gaskell

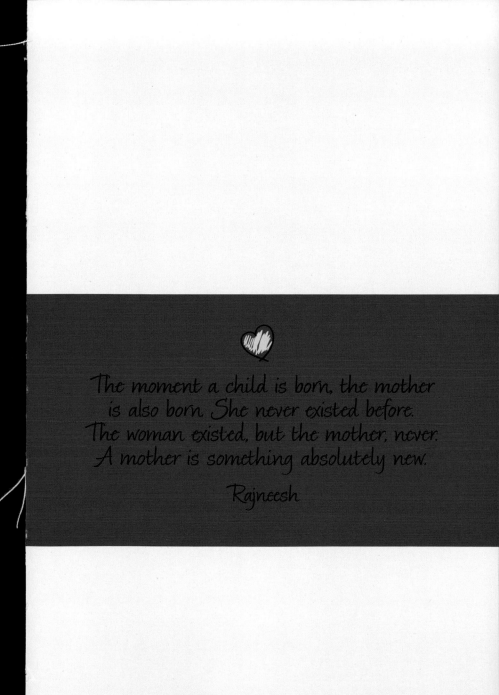

The moment a child is born, the mother
is also born She never existed before.
The woman existed, but the mother, never.
A mother is something absolutely new.

Rajneesh

Most of all the other beautiful things in life come by twos and threes, by dozens and hundreds. Plenty of roses, stars, sunsets, rainbows, brothers and sisters, aunts and cousins, comrades and friends—but only one mother in the whole world.

Kate Douglas Wiggin

If you've never been hated by your child,
you've never been a parent.

Bette Davis

Thanks, Mom, for teaching me how to bait a fishhook and then how to cook the fish we caught.

Thanks, Mom, for never being too busy
to play soccer with me, to bake brownies
with me, to just sit and cuddle with me.

Motherhood is still the biggest gamble in the world. It is the glorious life force. It's huge and scary—it's an act of infinite optimism.

Gilda Radner

Though motherhood is the most important
of all the professions—requiring more
knowledge than any other department in
human affairs—there was no attention
given to the preparation for this office.

Elizabeth Cady Stanton

For the hand that rocks the cradle
is the hand that rules the world ...

William Ross Wallace

Thanks, Mom, for growing strawberries
in the garden.

I'm thankful motherhood brings
wonderful new people into my orbit.

Life is always a rich and steady time
when you are waiting for something to
happen or to hatch.

E. B. White

Our mothers remain the strangest,
craziest people we've ever met.

Marguerite Duras

I'm thankful motherhood involves play dates with other moms and dads.

Youth fades; love droops;
the leaves of friendship fall;
A mother's secret hope
outlives them all.

Oliver Wendell Holmes

Women's rights in essence is really a movement for freedom, a movement for equality, for the dignity of all women, for those who work outside the home and those who dedicate themselves with more altruism than any profession I know to being wives and mothers, cooks and chauffeurs, and child psychologists and loving human beings.

Jill Ruckelshaus

Thanks, Mom, for waiting up for me when I was out late—I know I complained, but secretly I really appreciated it.

Thanks, Mom, for making the big world
out there a less scary place, because
I know you're in it.

Mother's love is peace. It need not be acquired, it need not be deserved.

Erich Fromm

I'm thankful motherhood gives me an excuse to eat chicken fingers again. Yum!

A father may turn his back on his child,
brothers and sisters may become
inveterate enemies, husbands may desert
their wives, wives their husbands. But
a mother's love endures through all.

Washington Irving

Thanks, Mom, for reading
"Goodnight Moon" so often
you can still recite it from memory.

A mother understands
what a child does not say.

Traditional proverb

If love is sweet as a flower, then my mother is that sweet flower of love.

Stevie Wonder

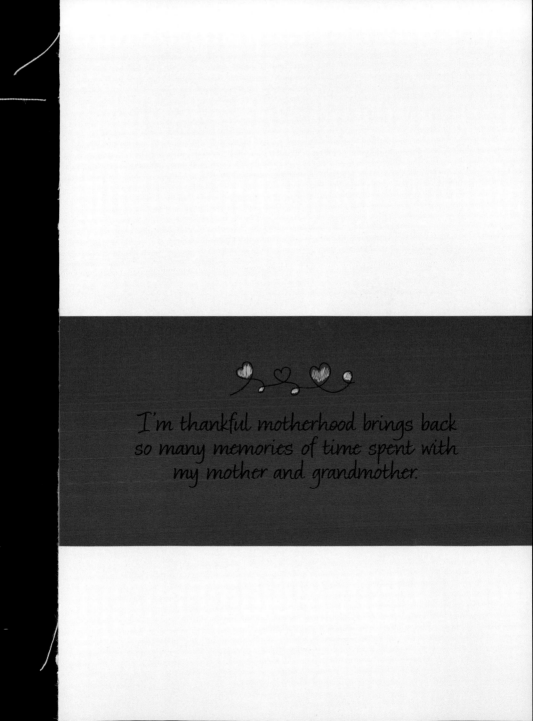

I'm thankful motherhood brings back
so many memories of time spent with
my mother and grandmother.

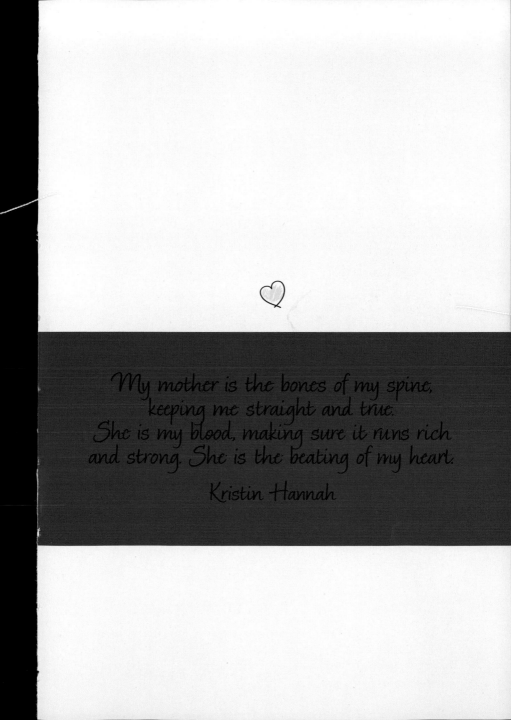

My mother is the bones of my spine,
keeping me straight and true.
She is my blood, making sure it runs rich
and strong. She is the beating of my heart.

Kristin Hannah

I'm thankful that motherhood introduces
new traditions to my family.

One of the oldest human needs is having someone to wonder where you are when you don't come home at night.

Margaret Mead

I'm thankful motherhood
gives me the chance to know the brilliant
people who are my children.

Thanks, Mom, for helping me to become
the best possible version of myself.

Don't poets know,
Better than others?
God can't be always everywhere:
And, so, invented Mothers.

Sir Edwin Arnold

Thanks, Mom, for loving me unconditionally.

I'm thankful motherhood
teaches me the true meaning of peace.

I'm thankful motherhood reminds me
how great the summer is.

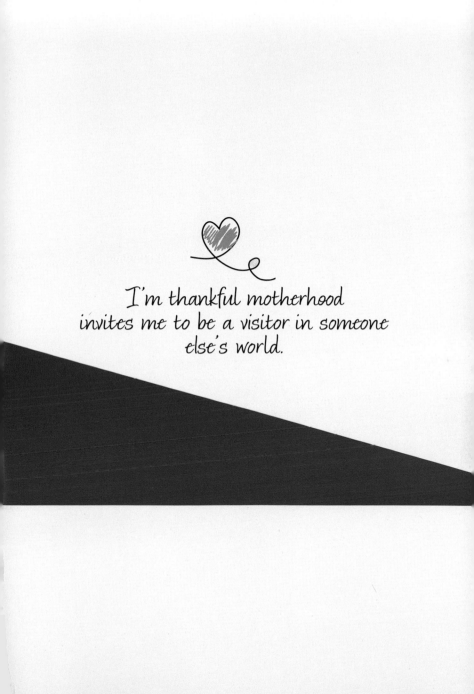

I'm thankful motherhood
invites me to be a visitor in someone
else's world.

About the Designer

The sculpture design in this edition was created exclusively for ArtFolds by **Luciana Frigerio**. Based in Vermont, Luciana has been making photographs, objects, book sculptures, and artistic mischief for over 30 years. Her work has been exhibited in galleries and museums around the world. Luciana's artwork can be found at: www.lucianafrigerio.com, and her unique, customized book sculptures can be found in her shop on the online crafts market Etsy at: www.etsy.com/shop/LucianaFrigerio.

The ArtFolds Portfolio

Color Editions

These smaller ArtFolds™ editions use a range of colors printed on each page to make each sculpture a multi-colored work of art. Titles now or soon available include:

Edition 1: Heart
Edition 2: Mickey Mouse
Edition 3: Christmas Tree
Edition 4: MOM
Edition 5: Flower

Classic Editions

These larger ArtFolds™ editions include the full text of a classic book; when folded, book text appears along the edges, creating a piece of art that celebrates the dignity and beauty of a printed book. Titles now or soon available include:

Edition 1: LOVE
Edition 2: Snowflake
Edition 3: JOY
Edition 4: READ
Edition 5: Sun

To see the full range of ArtFolds editions, visit www.artfolds.com.